PIGS APLENTY, PIGS GALORE!

DAVID MCPHAIL

Puffin Books

PUFFIN BOOKS

Published by the Penguin Group

Penguin Books USA Inc., 345 Hudson Street, New York, New York 10014, U.S.A.

Penguin Books Ltd, 27 Wrights Lane, London W8 5TZ, England

Penguin Books Australia Ltd, Ringwood, Victoria, Australia

Penguin Books Canada Ltd, 10 Alcorn Avenue, Toronto, Ontario, Canada M4V 3B2

Penguin Books (N.Z.) Ltd, 182-190 Wairau Road, Auckland 10, New Zealand

Penguin Books Ltd, Registered Offices: Harmondsworth, Middlesex, England

Copyright © 1993 by David McPhail

Library of Congress number 92-27986

ISBN 978-0-14-055313-0

Published in the United States by Dutton Children's Books,

a division of Penguin Books USA Inc.

Published in Great Britain in Puffin Books 1997

Designer: Riki Levinson

Manufactured in China by RR Donnelley Asia Printing Solutions Ltd.

First Puffin Edition 1996

For Jack,
good friend, true poet

Late one night
As I sat reading,
I thought I heard
The sound of feeding.

Through the kitchen door
I crept,
Barely watching
Where I stepped.

A crash, a bang,
A shout, a yell—
I slipped on something,
Then I fell.

I landed on
A pile of pigs—
Some eating dates,
Some eating figs.

In the cupboards,
On the floor—
Pigs aplenty,
Pigs galore!

Black pigs, white pigs,
Brown and pink,
Making oatmeal
In the sink.

Pigs in tutus,
Pigs in kilts,
Pigs on skateboards,
Pigs on stilts.

Pigs from England,
Pigs from France,
Pigs in just
Their underpants.

The King of Pigs,
The Piggy Queen—
The biggest pigs
I've ever seen.

Pigs arrive
By boat, by plane.
A bus pulls up
And then a train.

A band strikes up.
A piggy sings.
Then, at ten
The doorbell rings.

Someone yells:
"The pizza's here!"
And all the pigs
Begin to cheer.

Flying pizzas
Fill the air.
One goes SPLAT!
Against my chair.

The piggy piggies
Eat their fill.
I get nothing,
Just the bill.

"I've had enough!"
I scream and shout.
"Get out, you pigs!
You pigs, get out!"

"Please let us stay,"
  The piggies cry.
"Don't make us go,
  Don't say good-bye."

"You can stay,"
  I tell them all.
"But sweep the floor
  And scrub the wall."

I give them brooms,
A pail, a mop.
"Now sweep and scrub
Till I say stop."

The piggies work
And when they're done,
Upstairs they stagger
One by one.

They brush their teeth
And comb their tails,
Then wash their snouts
And clean their nails.

The pigs and I
Climb into bed.
I plump the pillows,
Plop my head.

Of pigs and pigs
And pigs some more—
Of pigs aplenty,
Pigs galore!

I close my eyes
And try to sleep.
Before too long
I'm dreaming deep—